JESUS AND THE BIG PICNIC
and other stories

© Three's Company/
Angus Hudson Ltd 1987
First published by Moody Press
c/o MLM,
Chicago, Illinois 60610,
U.S.A.

ISBN 0 8024 8488 3

All rights reserved. No part of this publication may be reproduced, stored in a retrieval system, or transmitted, in any form or by any means, electronic, mechanical, photocopying, recording or otherwise without the prior permission in writing of Three's Company/Angus Hudson Ltd

Created and produced by Three's Company, 12 Flitcroft Street, London WC2H 8DJ

Worldwide co-edition organized and produced by Angus Hudson Ltd

Design: Peter M. Wyart
Illustration research: Christine Deverell
Typesetting by Watermark

Jesus and the Big Picnic
and Other Stories

Stories retold by Tim Dowley; illustrations by Richard Deverell

Contents

Water into Wine
Jesus and the Tax-man
Stories by the Seaside
The Big Picnic
Man up a Tree!
Blind Man Sees!

Water into Wine

Once there was a wedding in a little village near the Sea of Galilee. Lots of people were invited – all the friends and relations of the bride and bridegroom. Jesus was invited too, with his mother Mary and his followers.

After the bride and groom had been married, there was a wonderful party. Everybody ate and drank and sang and danced for days and days. But on the third day Mary came to Jesus:

'The wine has all gone – but the guests are still thirsty. Can you help?'

And Mary said to the servants:

'Do whatever Jesus tells you.'

There were some huge pots standing in the room. So Jesus said to the servants:

'Fill up those pots with water.'

So without asking any questions the servants filled the pots right up to the brim.

Then Jesus said:

'Now pour some out and take it to the host of the party.'

The servants did just as he told them, and the host tasted the water that had been turned into wine. But as soon as the host tasted it, he called to the bridegroom:

'Everyone always brings out the best wine at the beginning of the party. They leave the cheap wine till later, when the guests have already had plenty to drink. So why have you saved the best wine till now?'

He didn't know that Jesus had turned the water into wine! This was the very first miracle that Jesus did.

Can you find?

You can find this story in John 2:1–11.

Now look at the picture
Can you find the musicians?
What instruments are they playing?
Where are the bride and bridegroom?
How many oil lamps can you find?
Point to a man with a jug of wine.
Find a man pouring water into a pot.
How many dogs can you see?

Something to do
Draw the bride and bridegroom tasting the new wine.

Jesus and the Tax-man

One day Jesus was walking through the town of Capernaum, beside the Sea of Galilee. By the road he saw a man called Matthew, sitting in his office with piles of money in front of him.

Matthew was a tax-collector. Many of the Jewish people hated him because he collected taxes for the Romans, who ruled the country with their soldiers. Sometimes he even kept some of the money for himself.

But when Jesus saw Matthew, he decided he wanted him as one of his special friends. So Jesus said to Matthew:

'Follow me!'

Matthew got up at once from his table and followed Jesus.

He was very glad to leave his job and follow Jesus and decided to have a great party to celebrate. So he sent out invitations to his friends – many of whom were tax-collectors too.

It was a wonderful party. There were crowds of guests, and Jesus and his friends came too. There was more than enough to eat and drink, and Matthew and his friends had a great time.

But some of the religious people gathered outside Matthew's house. They had heard that Jesus was at Matthew's party.

'Why are you eating and drinking with a bad man like Matthew?' they asked Jesus.

Jesus had a sort of riddle for an answer:

'Healthy people don't need a doctor – but sick people do. I came to call bad people – not people who think they're already good.'

Can you find?

You can find this story in your Bible in Matthew 9:9–13.

Now look at the picture

What can you see in Matthew's office?
How many lambs and sheep can you count?
Point to the baskets of fish.
Can you find some fishing boats?
Can you find a man selling cloth?
Point to the potter at his wheel.

Something to do

Draw a picture of Matthew at his party.

Stories by the Seaside

One day Jesus was talking to his friends beside the Sea of Galilee. More and more people came to hear what he had to say, until the crowd grew enormous. Then Jesus had an idea.

'Launch this boat,' he said to his friend Peter. 'I will sit in the boat and talk to the people from there.'

So Peter and his friends rowed Jesus out a little way onto the water and let down the boat's anchor. Then Jesus began to tell the people a story:

'Listen! There was once a farmer who went out to sow seed. As he sowed, some seed fell on the path, and birds came and gobbled it up. Some seed fell on stony places. This seed sprang up quickly, because there wasn't much soil. But when the sun shone, the shoots withered because they had no roots. Some seed fell among thorns, and the thorns grew up and choked the plants.

'But some of the farmer's seed fell on good ground. This seed sprang up and produced a good crop of grain, with many ears of wheat.'

When the people had gone home, and Peter had rowed Jesus back to the shore, Jesus' friends said to him:

'We enjoyed your story. But we don't really understand what it means!'

So Jesus said to them:

'It's like this. People who hear what God is saying to them, and do as he says, are like good ground that produces good things.'

Can you find?

You can find this story in Mark 4:1–20.

Now look at the picture
Can you find Jesus in the boat?
Point to the farmer sowing his seed.
Can you find men building boats?
Can you find any sick people?
How many baskets of fish can you count?
How many donkeys can you find?

Something to do
Try growing mustard and cress seeds. You can buy them in a packet and grow them on damp blotting paper. They grow very fast.

The Big Picnic

So many people were coming to see Jesus that he and his followers didn't even have time to eat. They were getting very tired. So Jesus said to them:

'Come with me, and we'll go somewhere quiet where we can rest.'

So they all got into a boat and sailed across the Sea of Galilee to a quiet place where nobody lived. But before they could land, people started arriving. They had seen Jesus leaving town and followed him round the shore. Soon there was a huge crowd of people.

Although he was tired, Jesus didn't send the people away but began telling them some of his special stories. Some of his friends came to Jesus:

'It's getting late, and we are far from home. Send the people away to find something to eat.'

But Jesus said:

'You give them something to eat.'
But they said:

'That would cost a huge amount of money. We can't afford it.'

So he said:

'How many loaves do you have?'

They went back to the crowd and asked how many loaves people had. But nobody had anything to eat. At last they found a little boy who had just five loaves and two fish.

Then Jesus told his friends to ask the people to sit down in groups. He took the five loaves and two fish that the boy had given him, thanked God, and broke the bread. Then he gave out the food to his friends, who gave it to the people. Everyone had plenty to eat – a good lunch of bread and fish. Even when everyone had finished, Jesus' friends picked up twelve baskets of leftovers.

Can you find?

You can find this story in John 6:1–13.

Now look at the picture
How many boats can you see?
Point to Jesus teaching.
How many animals can you find?
Point to a boy up a tree.
How many loaves can you find?
Can you find any fish?

Something to do
Draw the boy giving his loaves and fish to Jesus' friends.

Man up a tree!

In the town of Jericho there lived a tax-collector named Zacchaeus. He was the chief tax-collector of the town and was a very rich man. He heard that Jesus was coming to Jericho and decided he wanted to meet him. He had heard a lot about Jesus, how he healed sick people, how he performed miracles, and how he told the people special stories.

Crowds of people in Jericho were all trying to see Jesus. Zacchaeus was only a little man. When Jesus arrived, Zacchaeus found he couldn't see over people's heads. He didn't catch even a glimpse of Jesus. In a moment he decided what to do. Zacchaeus climbed up a sycamore-fig tree by the roadside. Once he'd reached the top he could see everything.

The crowd was very close, with Jesus right in the middle. Zacchaeus had a perfect view. But just as Jesus reached Zacchaeus' tree, he stopped. He looked up into the tree:

'Zacchaeus, come down at once! I want to stay at your house today.'

Zacchaeus was down the tree before another word was said.

'You will be very welcome at my house today,' he told Jesus.

Because he was a tax-collector, and many people thought he was a cheat, some in the crowd asked why Jesus would go to his house. Zacchaeus heard what they were saying:

'Look, Lord!' he said. 'Here and now I give away half of everything I have to the poor. If I have cheated anybody, I will give them back four times as much in repayment.'

And Jesus said to him:

'Today salvation has come to your house, Zacchaeus!'

Can you find?

You can find this story in Luke 19:1–10.

Now look at the picture
Can you find Zacchaeus in the tree?
Point to a Roman soldier on his horse.
Point to a woman grinding grain.
Find a well in the picture.
Point to a woman sewing.
Where is Jesus in the picture?

Something to do
Draw a picture of Zacchaeus collecting taxes in his office.

Blind Man Sees!

Jesus and his followers had come to the town of Jericho. Now they were leaving. Many people followed, wanting to see Jesus. A blind man called Bartimaeus was sitting by the side of the road. He sat there every day, begging from passers-by. He heard the voices of the crowd.

'Why are there so many people?' he asked. 'What's going on?'

A man standing nearby said:

'Haven't you heard? Jesus of Nazareth is coming. That's why there are so many people.'

As soon as he heard that Jesus was coming, Bartimaeus called out:

'Jesus! Jesus, have mercy on me!' People turned round.

'Stop shouting! Don't make all that noise. Shush!!'

But it didn't make any difference. Bartimaeus called out even louder:

'Jesus! Jesus of Nazareth, have mercy on me!'

Jesus heard him shouting. He stopped.

'Call him!'

So they said to Bartimaeus:

'Cheer up! On your feet! He's calling you!'

So Bartimaeus jumped up, threw off his cloak, and rushed towards Jesus. Jesus asked him:

'What do you want me to do for you?'

'Lord Jesus, I want to see!'

'Go your way!' said Jesus. 'Your faith has made you well again.' Immediately Bartimaeus' eyes were opened. Leaping for joy, he followed Jesus down the road.

When all the people saw what had happened, they gave thanks to God.

Can you find?

You can find this story in Mark 10:46–52.

Now look at the picture

Can you find two Roman soldiers?
How many sheep can you find?
Point to the camels.
How many beggars can you see?
Which man is Bartimaeus?
Can you find a man up a tree?

Something to do

Draw Bartimaeus sitting beside the road begging.